ACTIONS HAVE CONSEQUENCES

Do things happen to us for a reason?

Are we responsible for the things that happen, or do they just happen?

Do the things that happen to us make us stronger or weaker?

Are we unlucky or do we make our own luck?

What affects do the things we do have on the people around us?

Do our actions have consequences?

ACTIONS HAVE CONSEQUENCES

HOW ONE MAN'S ACTIONS ALTERED
THE LIVES OF SEVERAL GENERATIONS

**A story based on the lyrics of 9 songs
written by the band FOURTOLD**

ERIC HELMSTETTER

For the members of the band,
for putting up with my lyrics that for some reason
always come out dark.

Acknowledgments

When Glenn Dlugosz (bassist) and I first started this project, our goal was simple, write some original music people like and scatter it into the set list of our north Jersey cover band TOXIC COCKTAIL. We decided to work outside the band with Brian Piper (guitarist) and Jim Cash (drummer) on a few song ideas and introduce fully finished songs back into our cover band's setlist. Neither of us had ever written songs with other people before, and I quickly realized this was where I'd rather focus my energy. Luckily Glenn agreed because none of this would have worked without him.

The ideas came quickly, and working together proved to be easier than I expected. Brian's open-mindedness and ability to hear through my basic cord structures and simplistic guitar parts made introducing songs so much more fun than I imagined. His approach to writing allowed everyone to stay in their own lanes and be the creator of their own parts. When we added Brian's catalog of songs that were looking for lyrics, it was obvious to me this project just wouldn't exist without Brian Piper. Before I knew it, we had 30 or so songs, and we were deciding on a band name.

FOURTOLD was born.

Every project needs a power source, and FOURTOLD'S is Jim Cash. He is our engine. He likes to say that I am the lead, but he is truly the person responsible for the energy that keeps this band running. There's no doubt in my mind if it wasn't for Jim, this project would have stalled long ago. His ideas are so far out of the box that it forces you to think of ways to get them back in. For me, that's an ideal situation.

As the lyricist and vocalist in the band, I wanted the songs to have an emotional connection with people. Emotion = Art. I would imagine all lyricists say that, but it's the truth; it is art. Maybe people don't refer to it as art because it's not something they can see. They listen to music, but they don't always watch a musical performance which I think separates them from the art. I didn't know it at the beginning, but Jim's persistence made it clear. He knew me better than I knew myself. Art would be the thing that separates our band from the millions of other small-town bands.

When I approached the band with the idea of connecting a few songs (nine to be exact) into one long story and then performing them as a narrated play, the decision was unanimous.

Actions Have Consequences - A narrated, animated play with live music by FOURTOLD.

Actions Have Consequences is based on 9 of our songs.

"I Know It's Me"

"Monday Mourning"

"Weak"

"End the Wait"

"Unwanted"

"She"

"Rain"

"Why Did You Leave"

"Actions Have Consequences"

The screenplay follows the story of 5 people whose lives were dramatically altered by the heinous actions of a single person:

All I needed to do was write an outline based on the ideas of each song and fill in the rest of the story. Simple right?

Outline. Easy.

Ideas and storyline. Easy.

Filling in content and conversation... Ahhh...Hmmm.

It was time to call a long-time friend for help flushing out the details of this story. He immediately said yes, and within a few months, we had our first draft. And then... someone close to him saw what he was working on and disagreed with the storyline. He was asked to stop working on the project. That's when I knew I had something truly powerful.

EMOTION = ART

He made the decision to continue writing even though it

caused tension in his life. He asked to stay anonymous. I wish he didn't, but I understand why he did.

So, I have a ghost-writer, and I'm happy I do because he nailed it. He really brought my vision to life.

To my ghostwriter directly, I am forever thankful for your friendship and for your involvement in this project.

I would also like to thank my editor Tristen Laferrier. Author of Black Haired Boy and Dear Brother. After I read Black Haired Boy, I knew he would really bring the conversations between characters to life.

About the Author

Eric Helmstetter is a creative mind, who stops at nothing to see an idea though to the end if it is of interest to him. Artist, Singer-Songwriter, Lyricist, Husband, Father, and Grandfather, Eric lives his life in northwestern New Jersey. The storyline behind this book came from the lyrics of nine songs that Eric co-wrote in his band FOURTOLD.

Chapter 1
The Corkscrew

Another night at a dive bar, Richard thinks to himself as he sits in the parking lot of The Corkscrew.

Looking in the rear-view mirror of his Buick LeSabre, he doesn't appreciate the intrusion of greys into his already-thinning hair. *What the fuck,* he thinks as he steps out of the car. *I'm only here for some peace and quiet, anyway.*

One more night in that house with his rotting corpse of a wife would be a bridge too far. Her latest idea… couples' therapy. *It will really help us, she says. Bob and Mary tried couples' therapy.*

Bob told me, *"Take responsibility for everything; otherwise you end up hashing and rehashing everything all the time. Take the blame, say you'll try harder, and you don't have to talk about it anymore."*

What could couples' therapy do for them? Could he really tell a total stranger how thoroughly he despised this woman he was married to? How all he could see was rolls of fat and drooping skin as she changed into her disgustingly ordinary 'old lady' wardrobe? How he was visually assaulted by iridescent red indentations where the elastic of her undergarments struggled to contain her ever-expanding girth?

She was a shapeless blob with pendulous, sagging breasts dotted by a constellation of moles and skin tags spread across her surface.

Ugh, I need a fucking drink, he thought to himself.

But was there really enough alcohol to wash away all this loathing?

Worth a try.

He walked up to the stoop.

…

So here he is at the corner of the bar, an all too familiar seat.

"I'll have a Manhattan," he says to the bartender.

This is Charlie, not his favorite, but it's Tuesday night. Beggars can't be choosers.

The interior of The Corkscrew is really kind of depressing.

The unspoken standoff between the down-and-out locals and the just-barely-of-age college students, the main ammunition expended being cold stares and sneers tinged with ridicule. A thick cloud of smoke hangs over the place like a fog causing the neon beer signs to glow a little more eerily in the dim light. Something has always felt a bit off about this place.

The jukebox alternates between the folk and rock music of the college kids and the more traditional fare preferred by the permanent residents.

A drink appears before Richard, and he clutches it tightly. He can feel it before he even puts the glass to his lips. The warm flush he anticipates, the welcome haze that helps him tolerate this life that confines him.

The trips to the bar are becoming more and more frequent. He's having a hard time lying to everyone these days and finds solace in the warm embrace of four or five stiff drinks.

He hears the musical strains of one of the songs the kids have been playing these days:

"A long, long time ago, I can still remember how the music used to make me smile…"

Christ, I'm in it for ten minutes now, this god-forsaken funeral dirge. Lionizing some washed up folksingers and hippie rockers. No thanks.

Richard surveys his compatriots down the bar. From his corner perch, he has a good view of the place. He sees someone directly across the bar staring straight through him. Who is this guy? Is he the father of one of Jimmy's friends? Someone from work? Where has he seen this guy?

Richard gives him a nod and goes back to the task of inventorying the crowd.

"Drove my Chevy to the levy, but the levy was dry..."

Richard remembers hearing a radio interview with the artist who indicated that this was some kind of reference to his own local watering hole.

He sips the last of the first drink of the night, Manhattan, concocted of whiskey and rye. Irony…

"Charlie hit me again." Richard slides a crumpled-up twenty across the bar.

…

He looks over to the guy from work/dad of his kid's friend/ stranger? There's that stare again. What is with this guy? He's beginning to feel uncomfortable now.

The next drink materializes; Charlie grabs the twenty and walks to the register.

An argument breaks out at the pool tables; apparently, there was some question of whether the correct pocket was called or some bullshit like that.

A girl jostles Richard on the way to the bar. She's a young college student and has to be underage, but the way she looks may just force Charlie to serve her anyway. She's trying to get some drinks for herself and two of her friends, who are huddled in the corner, trying to avoid detection.

Charlie looks around at the young, pretty waitresses in the bar, and sees the strong-looking busboys, most with their close-cropped hair carrying trays heaping with empty glasses, uneaten food scraps, and piles and piles of plates. He follows one of these plate-piles past the staring guy, who is staring yet again.

A seething rage is stirring within him.

Drink number two is going down way too easily and Richard is trying to flag Charlie down for his third.

He starts to think, though he hates when that happens. Thinks back to when he was much, much younger. He was kind of a chump even then. Secondary school dances. He would watch Theresa Hudson milling around the edges of the dance floor, always trying to work up the nerve to ask her to dance, but would inevitably, begrudgingly agree to dance with Michelle, the pimply, overweight, bad-smelling mess of a cunt.

Fast-forward twenty-five years, he's now married to Michelle. Well, not Michelle, but might as well be.

...

The third drink arrives; Charlie rifles through the change at the bar's edge and grabs just enough to cover this one. Looking up, he sees the back of the staring guy's head as he slips into the crowd, ostensibly on his way to the restroom. Richard grabs the glass and downs it in one gulp as he heads to the bathroom to confront this guy. Weaving his way through the throng of people out of the corner of his eye, he sees the door swing shut.

Just then, the marathon song ends, and another starts up. This one is much more to Richard's liking, a local band that is getting some play.

"There's a mad, mad side of me…"

Richard doesn't really catch all the words, but the sound speaks to him instinctually in some way

At the bathroom door, he looks furtively around the bar just to see if anyone was headed his way. All clear, he enters the room and runs chest-first into the guy. Flustered and unsure of what to do next, Richard grabs him, two fistfuls of the shirt where the lapels would have been had he been wearing a coat.

"What the fuck do you want?! Who are you?!"

Richard screams into the stranger's face just inches away from his own.

The stranger doesn't seem surprised by this aggressive tone

and gazes back almost passively at Richard.

There is a rush of blood to his face, a hum in his ears that drowns out the rest of the world. He becomes disoriented as the dated, paneled bathroom spins around him. The most recent drink is gurgling up in the back of his throat.

He looks at this guy, who he doesn't know, and sizes him up a bit. He shifts his weight to his right leg and staggers back slightly to gain some balance; lets go with one of his hands, and then…

leans in…

starts to…

…kiss this man, full-on on the lips.

He feels an exhilaration consume his entire body, a foreign arousal that has manifested in a sort of electricity tingling through his very being.

The kiss lasts what seems to be a long time but it has probably only been seconds until Richard regains control of himself.

What am I doing, he thinks to himself. This is not who I am. Who is this creep standing so close to me? Why did he kiss me?

Deep down, Richard knows he instigated this entire interaction.

Who does he think he is? Why is he standing there with that self-satisfied smile? What kind of fucking pervert kisses a total stranger?

His eyes are feeling bloodshot; a boiling pressure is on his temples. Sweat is seeping from his brow.

Richard takes stock of where he is standing, this disgusting bathroom with the yellow puddles at the base of the urinals.

Who the fuck can't hit a urinal, and these are those fucking floor to mid-chest sized urinals too. What is wrong with people?

He sees the piles of used paper towels in the corner spilling out of the garbage can, the streaked mirrors with effortless, vulgar graffiti scrawled across them, the dank smell of bad cologne, days' old urine sticking between the tiles, stale beer remnants in cups and bottles propped around every horizontal surface, smoke clouding that makes his skin crawl.

He looks back at this guy, a sense of revulsion taking over him. The self-satisfied smile is starting to look like something more sinister. Words are coming out of the guy's mouth, but Richard is not receiving them. There is still a kind of hum echoing around in his head, though his other senses have sharpened into an almost uncomfortable focus. Richard's left hand is still grasping the imaginary lapel of the stranger's shirt.

Richard cocks his right hand back and swings wildly, hitting the confused stranger right below his left eye. He feels the solid contact of his fist, and the guy's cheekbone as the last two knuckles of his hand make some kind of popping sound. Still holding tightly to the shirt, he twists his left hand to get more leverage and fires another shot into the bewildered man's forehead. This punch really hurts his already-swelling right fist. Unable to properly recoil because of his left hand and losing his footing in one of the aforementioned urine puddles, the victim starts falling to the floor, accidentally avoiding an uppercut from Richard's bruised and swelling fist.

One more shot to the ear on the way down, and the man is on the floor, awkwardly falling between a stall and the urinal's privacy guard. Richard steps back, surveying this pathetic creature scrambling to try to get up from this untenable position, his head hanging beyond his shoulders as his feet and arms flailing for purchase.

Richard steps forward and plants a solid kick right to the side of the man's face, followed by a stomp on his chest.

"Get out of here!"

Richard's inner voice screams to him as he glances erratically around the room. He darts to the exit, grabs the trash can by the door, and hurls in the direction of the beaten man rolling slowly to his back.

Richard beats a hasty retreat to the exit out into the cool, night air. His head is spinning now, more so than in the lead-up to that degenerate pervert trying to kiss him in the bathroom.

The adrenaline rushes through him, his heart pounding out of his chest. His breathing is rapid, but controlled.

What have you done?

...

What is wrong with you?

The brisk autumn air is starting to bring him back to his senses.

I've got to get home. Ugh, home. Got to get some ice on this hand. Got to get out of these dirty, smoky clothes. The cunt's going to be all over me.

"Where have you been?!" " What were you doing?!" "Who were you with?!"

I've never seen that guy before in town. He probably doesn't know me. Everything kind of happened fast and I did give him kind of a walloping. Maybe he'll have trouble identifying me. Is this a rip in my shirt? How did that happen? Am I like those guys that drive slowly through the park

No I'm not a weirdo.

I'm totally normal.

...

But that kiss...it felt so good, so right.

Chapter 2
This Isn't Working Out

Ugh…she's down there screaming again.

They always scream like someone is going to come and help her.

Believe me, I know. It's like when you're at the Home Store. Some guy is struggling to get a 4x8 sheet of plywood into the back of a minivan by himself. Drywall is the best. They end up breaking all the corners, twisting it one way or the other to try to get it past the tapered opening for the door. Probably thirty people walk right past this poor asshole, vainly attempting to secure it just enough to drive the five miles home, where they will mess it up even more with their ridiculous do-it-yourself "skills."

I know. I work there. I have the stupid red vest with *"James"* scrawled in Sharpie marker across it.

Anyway, she's down there expecting the guy who won't step up and grab the back end of a sheet of building material for a grateful fellow human to suddenly bust the door down and go all Jack Bauer on. God only knows what's on the other side of said door. That is not going to happen.

Yet she still screams. I guess there's not much else for her to do. I remember the first time and how this all really freaked me out then; feeling nervous and scared that I'd be found out. By now, though, it's just more of a nuisance. This house isn't that big or remote, but no one is coming to help anyone.

Look, I don't want to hurt anyone. I'm just trying to make contact with another human. It's hard to make a connection these days with all that internet stuff. I don't look that good on paper, and honestly, my photo ain't stopping anyone from scrolling. If someone could just take the time to know me. I think I could get somewhere.

"I don't know."

I just want her to give me a shot. If she spent enough time with me, maybe she would realize that I'm not such a bad guy. Kind of like that stupid show my mom got all excited about when I was a kid. That furry, hideous dude captures that hot geeky girl, and after a few days in captivity, she falls in love with him. Not in that *"I'm a prince and have lots of wealth and a castle"* way, but a real deep connection way. Sure, I don't have singing and dancing furniture or anything, but I'm not hideous. Better than that dude, anyway.

That is not going to happen with this one. She spit at me and tried to scratch me the last time I loosened her wrists. No, this one has to go. It's a shame, really.

I remember the first time I had to take care of one of them. What a shitshow.

You know, in the movies, how someone sneaks into a hospital bed and throws a pillow over a person's face, applies a little weight to the center of the pillow, and after a few thrashes and kicks, that person goes off quietly? Well, it's not like that.

I remember being a kid and having to give pills to my cat. The first time I held him down, slipped the pill in there, then held his mouth closed until the pill went down. Well, I had to let go before that happened because that stupid cat was tearing the skin off both of my arms, spitting the pill out on the ground, and running under the couch.

Same thing. Like I said, shitshow.

I've since found a better way, but after that first time, it took me days to get back to normal. Well, I guess everyone has a different definition of "normal."

It wasn't always this way. There was a time when I had hopes, dreams, and friends. But that's all changed. That's all history.

I know who changed it, and I hate that motherfucker for changing it, but he's dead now. I didn't do it, wasn't there when it happened, wouldn't matter much if I did or didn't anyway because it wouldn't have unbroken me.

Whatever.

Anyway, it's a lot easier now. I don't have to hear all the screaming, begging, and crying, the kicking and the scratching, the cursing, and bargaining. None of it. They just go quietly. Then I just have to take out the trash.

It could be so much better than this. I move them in, and we talk for a while and get to know each other; things are cool. I could move them from the basement to the room without the door, then later into Mom and Dad's room. Well, my room now. Then who knows? Maybe we break up and go our separate ways, maybe we get married and have kids and a dog and all that nice stuff. That would be so much better than all this cursing and crying, spitting, and screaming.

But anyway, this one's got to go. She's not going to work out.

I guess after work today; I'll swing past the liquor store. I wonder if that cashier will be there, the one who is so damn talkative. Always like *"what's new with you?"*, *"did you have a good weekend?"*, *"you live near here?"*.

Strikes me as a bad judge of character. What's her name, Laurie or Laura or something like that? Ugh, kind of creeps me out.

But then, when I get home, I take care of her, clean up tomorrow, and we analyze what I did wrong and try to improve for the next time. I haven't really made any progress to speak of. No progress to not speak of, either. I don't know. This whole thing doesn't seem to be working the way I had hoped. Maybe my father was right about me. Maybe I am a failure. Everything I touch turns to shit.

I guess I learned from the best, right? That man was no prize. No father of the year. I guess there wasn't much chance of me being anything more than I am. Christ, I'm lucky to have made it this far.

2 am. I should get to bed. Have the early shift tomorrow. The contractor rush hits from 7 am to about 9 am. I hate those

assholes. After that, it's mostly the suburbanites buying yard waste bags, a single 2 x 3 that they ask you to cut down for them to exact measurements, grass seed for that fall seeding, four screws, and nonsense like that.

"The first piece I need to be two feet, three and five-eighths inches, the second one is two feet three and a half inches, and that's all I need. You can keep the leftovers."

I tell them that I have to charge for the second cut. They don't seem to care. What do-it-yourselfer doesn't have a saw? I could understand asking me to rip a sheet of plywood but a 2 x 3?

…

Lying in bed, chasing sleep, James' thoughts start to go to that dark place again. Imagining the light from the hallway under his bedroom door, seeing the shadow of feet beneath. He rolls over and puts his head under the pillow.

She's still down there screaming…

THIS ISN'T WORKING OUT

Chapter 3
316 Pine Street

Richard sits in his LeSabre on Maple street, a block or two from his house on Pine. His right hand is starting to swell, and it hurts to flex his fingers, especially his ring finger and the pinkie.

He sits in the car, reflexively opening and closing his fist, running the events of the night through his head. He's not really a fighter; he can't remember a single altercation since Ted Butz punched him in the mouth in the 8th grade. He actually had it coming, too.

Interesting, he thought. Boys and men are forced to moderate their behavior around other boys or men because of the threat of physical violence. When Ted was ripped by the coach and sent to the showers early, he didn't need to have a young Richie getting in his face and taunting him. A short jab to the upper lip put an end to that quickly.

Women do not live under that same threat. Well, some do, though society frowns on that kind of violence. But a guy belting another guy who crossed a polite social line? No problem. Go about your business.

This is why women become such shrews. That cow can say whatever she wants to me with no repercussions. She just crows on and on with zero risk and zero ramifications. Oh, to one day just pop her in the kisser while she's going on about which rag is for surfaces and which is for spills or how I use too many napkins. The look on her face as she starts to taste the blood from her cut lip. It would be magical. But I can't do that? There are rules against that.

The pain from Richard's possibly broken hand strangely gives him comfort. He thinks about the kiss and how it was better than anything he has experienced with his awful "wife." Even in the most modest of environments, that kiss was almost transformative.

He was briefly lifted out of his miserable existence into a world of possibilities. But then he went and messed that up, too.

Why did I hit that guy?

What came over me?

Can't go back to the Corkscrew for a while, I suppose. That's okay; there is plenty of holes in the wall downtown. I can always go across the way to The King's Corner or down the street to Guliana's. Anything's better than being "home."

He looks at the car's clock. 11:57. Well, it's actually only 10:57. He hadn't rifled through the glove compartment yet to find the LeSabre's manual to figure out how to switch the clock back to Standard Time. Or was it Daylight Savings Time?

I know you hold this button, or is it that button, then turn the tuning knob for the radio, or is it the volume?

He'll just continue to use the (currently displayed time - 1 hour = current time) formula for now.

Why do they have to make it so hard?

…

Richard envisions the living room of his depressing house.

All the lights are off; there is a glow from the television lighting the room. She's probably sitting in that ratty chair waiting for the local news to start, waiting for Jim Gardner to come on and authoritatively tell her about the most concerning events that happened in the nearby metro center that will have no impact or effect on her life whatsoever. She'll sit there and lap it all up as if it is significant, even though yesterday there was a similar story about a boy this time who vanished, or was killed playing with his father's gun, or fell into the family pool, or wandered out into the street. It's as if she soaks in all this tragedy to avoid the disaster that is in our lives.

"My marriage may be crap, but at least my husband didn't kill me and dispose of me in a mattress at the dump. My life is better

than that person's life."

If only there was a way to get past her and up the steps without her noticing anything. I could clean myself up and fall into bed and pretend for another seven hours that she didn't exist.

But I will not be so lucky, not tonight. Might as well get it over with.

He puts the car into drive and winds his way down Maple Street. Looking at houses he's driven past thousands of times before, and he wonders what secret wars are taking place behind each door on this street.

There's Steve's house.

I wonder if he and Sally are muttering under their breath every time they pass each other in the hall, or secretly flipping the other off behind a wall or piece of furniture. Do they start to pray that there was some fatal accident involving their spouse every time one of them is five or more minutes late coming home from the mall, or errands or work or something?

There's Gus's house.

Do you think Wanda secretly hates him for being transferred here for work, moving her away from her sister, and her college town, a place where she had connections and friends and activities? Taking her away from her favorite yoga studio, coffee shop or spin class? Starting over after 40 in a new town can get quite lonely.

There is a house of someone Richard does not know. What is the reason that the unknown wife in that house harbors a grudge against her unknown partner? There's got to be something. Same with the residents of 241 Maple as well as those at 240 just across the street.

The stop sign at Pine approaches.

Right or left? If I go left, that leads to my house, my driveway, my wife, my kid, and my prison. If I go right, that leads to a whole world of possibilities. I could start over. I could do something else, be someone else. I could breathe.

Who am I fucking kidding? I'm not courageous enough to

take that kind of leap. I'm going to fall in line, do what I'm supposed to do, and slowly drink myself to death like the rest of the residents of this suburban hellscape.

"Think of Jimmy. We don't want him to have issues forming relationships later in life. We have to stay together for him."

For him? What has that kid ever done for me?

I didn't even want kids. Certainly not him. I swear this monstrous woman intentionally got pregnant to keep me in this scenario. She told me repeatedly that doctors diagnosed that she was unable to have children due to her undiagnosed endometriosis and that there was so much scar tissue within her uterus that no fertilized egg would implant. She was effectively infertile.

Probably just another lie that she told to further entrap me. I have been married to her for eleven years. She and I have had sex three times in those eleven years, and one of those acts produces a child? In a scarred and damaged uterus? Please.

I have friends who pay thousands of dollars for fertility treatments just for the chance to have a baby. I'd pay thousands not to have a child. Children do not improve an empty and loveless marriage. Children do not take the pressure off middle managers who need to fight tooth and nail to keep from being passed over by more energetic and much younger coworkers. Children do not make nights and weekends easier.

When I was younger, I used to fear the inevitable end of my existence. I would lay awake in bed and stare wide-eyed at the ceiling, panicked about the presence or lack of existence of an afterlife. I would try to imagine what vast emptiness would come next, if any. I would cry at the thought of a world in which I did not exist anymore.

Now, I welcome the prospect of an end to everything, a time when there is no one depending on me for anything. It would be a peaceful, endless sleep. It sounds so wonderful.

One more gentle curve and his headlights would shine straight into the sitting room of his house at 316 Pine Street, a space that he calls "the museum" since no one has entered it in years. The furniture remains un-sat-on, the coffee table continues its coffee cup-free streak, and all the framed pictures adorning the walls are still unlooked at.

He parks at the end of the driveway and walks up the gentle slope to the house. Walking past the gardens lining the drive, he sees weeds choking out the flora that he so carefully planted when they first bought this place nearly a decade ago: the hostas choked out by pigweed, the patches of crabgrass lining the far edge of the gardens, the Creeping Charlie that has replaced most of his Kentucky Bluegrass yard much like his own deteriorating body and psyche.

He used to care about the house, the property, himself, and his relationship. All of that has since been beaten out of him by a series of indignities that he has been forced to tolerate. They started small, giving up some minor goals or desires like eliminating an inconvenient friend or two or avoiding those that she just did not think were "right" for him. They've since gone all the way to the current state, where he has given up any independent thoughts. It is a challenge now to determine where Richard ends and where his wife begins. It's as if they have become assimilated.

How does this happen? How does a man just disappear? I used to be a MAN, a fucking individual. I was a sentient being with thoughts and impulses of self-preservation and individuality. I have become a vessel, a husk that is built to serve others, a container for outsiders to pour their wishes into. I now live to serve others, subjugating any of my own wants in favor of people I don't even like. Don't respect.

Don't...

Richard opens the torn screen door. It's been that way for more than a year. He even has the replacement screen somewhere in the garage but can't muster the desire to get all the necessary tools out to pop the door off its hinges, remove all the remnants of the old screen, and replace it with the new one.

Come to think of it, the door kind of needs painting as well.

He shoves his right hand in his pocket to extract the keys and winces a bit at the pressure on the back of his damaged hand. He is instantly transported back to the men's room at the Corkscrew, to a time when he felt something again. Maybe he can feel that once more. Maybe there is a way for him to become so dominant again and not this nebbish fool who is taken advantage of at every turn.

I am a lion; he thinks as he inserts the key into the front door lock. He hesitates before giving it a turn.

Chapter 4
Men Are Worthless

My mom and her "friend" are fighting again.

April put on her headphones and turned the music up. *Why do they have to fight all the fucking time, my mom and this faceless, nameless guy, one in a string of men that have marched in and out of our life?* This one is not the worst. Carl was the worst.

Her mother's relationships have a pattern to them. April can see that this one is winding down. Being together day after day makes them worse all the time. The resentment they feel toward each other is palpable, the cold exchanges, the seething hatred that punctuates each sentence. They are becoming the worst versions of themselves. This one probably has three weeks, maybe a month to go.

Mom needs something, a room painted, plumbing work, furniture moved, whatever. She meets a guy, often from the store, he comes here, does the job for her, hangs around for another few weeks until she drives him away. Then there are stretches where it's just Mom and me again until the dryer conks out, the car needs an oil change.

She tells me, *"April, don't ever depend on a man for long-term plans. Get what you need from them and get rid of them. Not a single one of them is worth anything."*

If they didn't give up on each other so quickly and tried to build individual lives on their own, and if Mom would just make sure there was enough room for me on the edges, we could all be happy... or happier.

CRASH

The sound of something breaking downstairs bleeds through

the din of April's "songs."

Why doesn't she just fucking kick him out? The two of us could just go back to the way things were; we could move on and forget that he ever existed.

My mom's "friends" give me the creeps.

This one has dead eyes.

Mom is fine. I know she loves me, but she's just so fucking weak. It's embarrassing. She thinks this avoidance of stable relationships with men makes her strong. It's just the opposite. I know something happened with my dad and her, but that was a long time ago. She should really just get over it.

I mean, I get that Mom is struggling to make ends meet, what with her lowly retail clerk's income, that this damsel in distress act is a way to help get by, and she's trading something else of value in some type of bizarre barter system…trading her ass for handiwork.

I wish she didn't have to do this. I wish she could get paid enough to cover all our expenses and maybe just a little bit more. It's such bullshit that these huge companies make tons of money on the backs of broken and beaten little people like my mom and like me, I'm sure someday. I'll never go to college at this rate. I wouldn't even know where to begin to consider going to college.

The mere thought of coming up with the fifty dollars to register for the SAT is so daunting I can't imagine expending the effort required to study for the test and actually taking it.

No, mine will be a future much like my mom's. I just hope I'm not shackled for life to a shitty job and a string of Mr. Fix.

SLAM

…

She hears the front door close, shaking the whole house. The engine of his car revs and tires squeal as he takes off down the street.

…

I suppose I should go check in on Mom, April thinks. She's usually all red-faced and watery-eyed after these go-rounds, blubbering about how she loves him, and wishes he was different. As if she ever loved one of these guys. Delusional.

Save it, Mom. He is who he is.

…

She knocks lightly on her mother's bedroom door and opens it slowly.

"Mom," she says gently. "Are you okay?"

She sees the form of her mother slumped over at the foot of her bed. She often looks defeated after the usual fights, but tonight her body shakes from uncontrolled sobbing.

"Mom, don't do this to yourself."

As April's Mom turns her head, April sees a purplish bruise forming under her mother's eye, coupled with blood running from her split upper lip.

"Mom!" April gasped. Did he hit you?

We have to call the police!"

She listened to her mother explain how he didn't really mean to hurt her, how it was kind of her fault, and how she won't let it happen again.

"Mom! You sound just like one of those battered women you see on the cop shows! Are you listening to yourself ?!"

…

"At least let me get you some ice and a rag."

April walks downstairs through the aftermath. This one looks like it was worse than those before. It seems like things have been escalating recently, and she isn't sure why.

…

April had just recently turned seventeen. Her goal is to reach eighteen, get a place of her own, and put this whole life behind her.

Get a shitty job, live on boxed rice and beans, mac and cheese, or ramen noodles.

Maybe Noah can move in with her, and they can share expenses, split that box of shells with white cheddar sauce, and make just enough money to almost make it. Spend thirty or so years grinding it out, getting just a little above water until the car craps out and wipes out all of their savings.

Maybe she gets knocked up, and that ordeal takes whatever other scraps they had saved. The cycle of hopelessness and poverty continues. But this child will be loved by both of them. There will be no empty, soulless black shark-like eyes staring back at this poor child by its father, or plumber, or small engine repair man. This child who never really had a chance. As a family, they will make the most of what little they have. Then they can scratch and claw their way back up until one of them is diagnosed with cancer or drops dead from heart disease. That life insurance policy they always talked about getting but never really materialized.

There is no hope of generational wealth, no chance of inheriting money or property from the missing pieces of her family. The future is bleak. Not apocalyptic desolation, but more of a long and endless road of frustration and futility.

...

Standing in front of the refrigerator, she fishes through the ice tray for some full-sized cubes. Nothing. She grabs a bag of frozen corn, reaches under the sink for a washcloth, then holds the corner under the faucet to moisten it slightly.

She turns to survey the kitchen and picks up the chair that had been toppled over. She grabs the broom from the corner and sweeps up the broken glass, and the broken plate shards from the stained linoleum like she's trying to pull together the pieces of her life.

She better get back to her mom. April grabs the corn and the rag and heads back upstairs. She hands her mom the makeshift first aid kit, then sits by her on the bed with her arm around her mother's small shoulders.

What a role reversal, she thought as she consoled her frail, hurting mother.

This moment was broken by the sounds of his car pulling back into the driveway, the crunching gravel, the motor's hum, and the muffled radio sounds emanating from within the vehicle.

Her mother stiffened.

April stood up with a start, her hackles raised.

…

"Just go to your room, her mother said. "It'll be okay."

April heard the front door creak open.

…

She retreated silently to her room.

Chapter 5
Out With The Old, In With The New

Well, that was easy, James thought. It wasn't always that way.

James thinks back to the first time.

She screamed, begging, crying with snot running down her face. Me, crying, apologizing, asking for forgiveness.

Then me swinging erratically with a hammer. Making a total mess of things. Creating horrific sounds, the once solid bone of her skull feeling soft and mushy now. Gurgling sounds came from what was left of the person she was.

Mopping and scrubbing the concrete for days, trying to clean up the remnants. After a while, deciding to just paint over the whole floor with epoxy paint. This one had color flecks throughout it that made the entire floor look kind of festive. He picked up five gallons from aisle 17, bay 023, on the floor.

Now the floor cleans up nicely. Nothing stains it. But really, things are not nearly so messy anymore. He has it down to a science.

Step one, pretend to have a change of heart. Go downstairs and talk with her; make it seem like you realized what a horrible mistake you've made. Tell her you're willing to pay the consequences for your actions. Offer to call the cops and wait with her there until they arrive. Play up the sob story that is your life. Unfortunately, it doesn't take that much exaggeration to make it sound genuinely pathetic. Get her to drop her guard.

Step two, convince her to have just one drink with you, and pull out the sealed bottle that you just bought from the store today.

Oh, the store today.

Running into Tori, not Lori or Laurie…Tori. Every time he goes in to that store, she stops him and asks all kinds of questions about how he's doing, what he's been up to, and how his job is.

Honestly, it's kind of exhausting.

Why does this girl treat him like he's normal? If he didn't know any better, he'd think she was flirting with him. She keeps looking downward, then with just her eyes looking up into his face, acting all innocent and demure. She's always laughing a little too hard at the ordinary things that he says, the "accidental" touch when she returned the $5.37 in change to him, the sustained eye contact. It was almost uncomfortable, the way her words kind of followed him out the door when she said, "see you next time, James."

It's a good sign you're probably drinking a little too much when the cashier at the liquor store knows you by name.

She's not unattractive, kind of sweet. Don't really know her story. I would, however, say she's a bad judge of character.

So, where was I?

Right, step two. Convince her to have one drink with me, toast to the new sense of responsibility that I am taking with my life. Open the brand new bottle from the liquor store bag, receipt, and all. Crack the tamper-proof lid right in front of her and fill the two frosted glasses with a healthy-sized shot.

Oh yes, don't forget the crushed-up muscle relaxers frozen to the inside of one of the glasses. That stuff works wonders. With the mixture of alcohol and pharmaceuticals, they tend to go limp and not really lose consciousness but just lose the will, desire, and ability to resist anything. He releases the restraints and helps them gently to the floor. With his weight balanced on his heels, knees on either side of her small shoulders, James looks down at this girl and thinks:

If only you could have seen past the kidnapping and confinement to see just what type of person I am, none of this would be necessary.

He gingerly takes her face in his hands and mutters a few words of apology to the uncomprehending, disconnected form below him.

He looks for some recognition in her eyes but sees only dilated pupils taking in a swirling world.

He moves his hands to her neck and feels the soft skin where her neck and shoulders meet, feels the gentle rhythm of her slowing pulse. Then he carefully wraps his fingers around her neck and brings his body weight down as leverage to restrict her airways. He holds this position for two to three minutes as his hands start to ache, his triceps burn, and his knees start to hurt on the nicely-painted floor.

He stares directly into her eyes as he can feel all that she was starting to fade, quietly slipping away without a struggle.

This gives him a sense of power, of dominance. This is a man who should be taken seriously, not cast aside by a society that values achievement, wealth, or fame. For a moment, this utter, self-loathing loser held the key to life and death for an unfortunate girl.

"It didn't have to be this way…"

Then a simple task of double or triple bagging the remains in several large contractor bags. Aisle 04, Bay 005.

It's kind of challenging to get the body bagged up once the rigor mortis sets in, but it's helpful to fold them in half before they get too stiff. Wrap 'em up with Gorilla Tape. Aisle 42, Bay 002. Take them to the trash compactor at work. Throw it in and be done with it. Hope that there is no discovery, but those contractor bags and gorilla tape are really durable, and the triple bagging means no smells or visual evidence.

For the next few weeks, he sees flyers with "Missing" portraits dotting the telephone poles and has to kind of ignore them as he walks past. He feels a little bad about the whole thing for a while, but honestly, they could have avoided their fate. Just give him a chance. He's really not that bad.

He walks into the living room and sits down. It's finally quiet in here. After nearly a week of continual screaming coming from the basement, it's kind of nice to have a little silence. But not too much silence because then he starts remembering again.

Being alone in his room, in the dark. The shadows from the

feet in the hallway light coming through under the door. The sound of his father's

slurred words. The creaking sound of the door as it slowly opens.

Stop it!

Maybe there's a game on, a movie, or some other distraction. James finds a hockey game. It's in the third period. The Sabres, down 3-2, have pulled their goalie in a last-ditch effort to score. What the hell is a Sabre anyway? I know a Saber is a sword, but Sabre? It must be a French thing. Fucking French.

The opposition stole the puck and got a breakaway. Their player took a shot from center ice that, seemingly in slow motion, with two or three Buffalo players desperately chasing after it also strangely in a kind of slow motion, tracked to the center of the net. The red light flashed, a siren sounded, and the Sabres' fate was sealed.

Serves 'em right, James thought. Fuckin' Sabres.

Hell of a distraction. That was all of two minutes and twenty seconds.

"I need a drink," James said to no one and lumbered into the kitchen. The bottle of Jameson was only down two servings. He poured a third over one of those big, round ice cubes that seem so classy but are a pain in the ass to make in that rubber ice cube tray with the lid on it. You have to fill the tray up to the tip of the opening, but if the sides aren't tight, the water leaks out all over the inside of the freezer and then freezes the tray to the freezer floor. Then you have to unplug the refrigerator and let the whole thing thaw out. You have to put all your food in a cooler until it can go back into the running refrigerator again.

All my food, he thought as he looked in the fridge. There is a jar of olives from a year ago or more, ketchup, mayo and mustard, one egg, lots of those soy sauce and mustard packets you get from the Chinese restaurant down the street, and not a heck of a lot else. Oh, the rest of the moo shu pork that she didn't finish on her last night on earth. James loved those little pancakes.

"Can't let this go to waste."

He started to eat with his fingers right out of the take-out container. Didn't even heat it up. The pancakes were getting a little dry, but still not bad. Washed it down with a gulp of Jameson, his thoughts turning to Tori, the cashier from the liquor store.

Is this an opportunity staring him in the face? All this time, he's trying to force resistant strangers into seeing something in him that may or may not be there when all along, there's someone who seems interested in him already.

It's worth a try, he thinks.

James grabs his keys and jacket and heads for the door.

Too soon for another bottle of whiskey…that would be a red flag. Guess I could just pick up a pack of smokes and some gum.

He walks down the front porch stairs with a slight bounce in his step, the unpleasant events of the earlier evening already behind him.

Chapter 6
Work Sucks

Richard wakes up alone in his bed, the sun already past the tops of the windows. His head pounding, his right hand aching, and suddenly the events of last evening come back to him in a furious assault. He remembers an argument with her. He couldn't really remember the details, but of course, she was mad, his ripped shirt, his injured hand, smelling of smoke and liquor while stumbling around the house until he was able to properly navigate the staircase.

He thought of his epiphany in the parked car on Maple last night. He needs to be more of a man. More of a lion, as he recalls.

This will start today. When I get to work, the domino effect of the change is going to start.

Holy shit! Work! What time is it?!

He hears only silence downstairs which means that James has probably already caught the bus to his middle school. That would make it after 9 am at the earliest.

Shit, where's my watch…9:45?! I haven't slept until 9:45 in twenty-five years! Got to call the office and let them know that I'll be late. I'll tell them that the kid is sick, and I have to take him to the doctor.

He lumbers down to the kitchen, grabbing the phone off the counter and sticking his finger in the "1" hole. He spins the dial clockwise to the 5:00 position and lets the dial spin itself back to the start. Then the "3" hole and rotates the dial again.

"Susan? It's Richard. The kid is sick again. I need to take him to the doctor's; I'll be in around lunch. Can you juggle my schedule for me?"

"Okay."

"Thanks, see you then."

Now to hit the shower. On the way, he makes a stop at the medicine cabinet, grabs two aspirin, throws the pills down, and forcibly swallows them. The chalky tablets catch in his throat. He grabs a glass and fills it with water from the faucet. He spills half of it down his face and chest, the other half dislodging the pills from their confinement.

He drops his clothes to the floor, turns the water on as hot as he can stand, and steps into the shower. He feels the rush of hot water over him, the dizziness beginning to subside.

…

Richard pulls into his company's parking lot. It's not quite lunch, so there are no close spots. Barely any spots at all. He ends up in the gravel section that was just recently acquired for overflow since the company was experiencing such rapid expansion. They have not gotten around to paving it just yet.

He walks across the gravel, muttering to himself, his loafers getting all dusty, a stone lodging its way into his shoe.

Doesn't this beat all? Richard thinks to himself as the autumn sun high in the sky beats down on the back of his neck.

This is no way for a lion to be treated, he thinks as he walks past the reserved parking spots. There's Joe's car, that guy has only been here like two years, and he's twenty-five feet from the front door. I'm going on fifteen and parked in the gravel lot, so far away I can't even see my fucking car. We'll have to rectify this as well.

He reaches out to open the door, his hand grabbing the large metal handle. He winces in pain, his hand burning from pulling the large, heavy glass door.

Gonna have to get that looked at, he decided.

Susan greets him as he walks through the door.

"Super busy," he says. "Is Albert in today? I really need to talk to him."

"With a client," she replies. "He'll be back after two."

"Oh, well, can you get me on his schedule?" Today!

…

Richard spends the next few hours at his desk daydreaming, pushing papers from one side of his desk to the other. He's still massaging his damaged hand and fuming about the amount of disrespect he is exposed to daily at this damn office.

"Albert better fix this."

As his appointment gets closer, Richard can feel his confidence ebbing away. He tries to muster the rage that he unleashed on that unsuspecting man in the Corkscrew bathroom, but he can't. He starts making a list of the points he will make to Albert just in case he gets nervous.

And now he's squirming in the chair across from Albert, setting his portfolio on the edge of Albert's desk. They have worked together for a decade or more. They've never really liked each other, but they've been able to work together without issue.

Richard feels that Albert has never truly respected him or appreciated him. But all that is going to change now. He is running through the pitch in his head when his boss derails his train of thought.

"Richie, what can I do for you?"

"W-well," Richard stammers. "You know I've been here a long time."

Albert's eyebrows raise.

"I deserve more than I'm getting from this company."

…

"I need a raise and a promotion," he continues, not as confidently or as convincingly as he would like.

"Let me stop you right there, Richie," Albert interjects. "Look, you're a good guy, but honestly, you're not really performing even at minimal standards. You are far and away the lowest-rated manager on my staff. Your name regularly comes up during my upper management meetings as a way for us to cut expenses. I've been sticking my neck out trying to keep you safe here, knowing you have a wife and young child.

Don't make this more complicated for me. I'm going to need you to work harder and do better, and maybe in six months, we can talk about an increase."

...

"I know this isn't what you want to hear, but you're going to have to be okay with this unless you are ready for the alternative."

Richard feels the temperature rising on the back of his neck once again, this time from a different source. His scalp starts feeling prickly. That hum is consuming the inside of his head again. He begins to calculate precisely how to make a graceful exit.

"I guess I didn't think this one through," Richard muses to himself. "I understand." He said.

He meekly tries to smile, grabs his portfolio, and walks to the door.

Chapter 7
On The Edge

April was up and out early the next morning. She didn't want to take the chance of seeing him in the kitchen as she downed her Pop-Tarts and chocolate milk. She laughed to herself.

"I have the diet of a fucking nine-year-old."

Grabbing her backpack and water bottle, she yanked her keys off the hook by the door and bolted outside with no destination in mind and nearly two hours to go until the school doors would even open.

Wandering around the streets, April was trying to determine if she would even attend school today. She walked past Noah's house for the second time; his Toyota Corolla was parked in front of the garage, but still no sign of life.

No wonder he always shows up at school all disheveled with bedhead, she thought.

Downtown, she walked past the closed-up shops and restaurants, marveling at how the town was quiet and calm. Not as depressing as you would think. Parts of this town were actually kind of cute. Unfortunately, there's a whole other side to the town that is decidedly not cute.

On that side of town, there seem to be more alleys. More graffiti, more garbage in the street, and more people wandering around with fewer places to go. This is where April goes to engage in what her guidance counselor, Ms. Ricks, describes as "risky behavior."

She hasn't really done anything wrong; just kind of walks that line, but she gets closer to the edge all the time. There are those times she filled in shifts for her friend, Ruth's older sister, at the "gentlemen's club." She didn't dance or anything; she wore a fairly modest outfit, just showing some skin, mainly legs, and shoulders, shoulders, and she was pretty good in those areas.

She got lots of attention on those nights and lots of tips. A few handsy guys, but nothing she couldn't handle. Plus, there were enormous men at each entryway that would protect her from anyone who went too far.

The job was simple. Deliver drinks from the bar to tables full of drunk, lonely, horny guys. Collect credit cards and receipts, laugh at their stupid, insulting jokes, pretend not to be repulsed by them, and cry all the way to the bank.

She would tell her mother that she was sleeping at Ruth's house. Ruth would cover for her, and Ruth's sister would meet up with her married boyfriend because his wife was out of town. It was a win-win.

There were other times, too, like the time she took her mom's car without asking and broke 100 mph on the freeway. There was the time she used a fake ID to go to the low-rent bars and made out with that fifty-year-old dude. She wouldn't let it get too far, and Christ, he was old enough to be her father, but he was friendly and kind and looked at her like she was a goddess. That felt good.

He was so nervous and tentative, and could you imagine if he found out that she was only seventeen? Oh fuck, he'd lose it. That's why she got out of there by pretending she had to use the ladies' room and beat it out the back door.

She had the memory of giving a sad, older guy a thrill, and she gave him something to think about when he was alone and feeling amorous. There is none of the messiness that comes with getting to know someone, the disappointment that comes from real flesh and blood, the inevitable letdown that comes when he doesn't text back for a few hours, cancels plans at the last minute, or just says the wrong thing at the wrong time.

That is how she feels about Noah. Sure, he's nice enough, and he tries really hard. He's just kind of dumb and directionless. Not that she's setting the world on fire. Hell, she is just this close to not graduating high school, but she is smart enough to barely get by.

Her mom always tells her that if she would just apply herself, she could do whatever she wanted. But, honestly, is that true?

Let's say she took the SATs and scored high enough to get into a good school. Would her mom make the sacrifices necessary for her to be able to really lean into a decision like that?

Not a fucking chance, she thought.

And so, she spends her time here split between being the good girl who does what is expected of her and being the thrill-seeker that gets her kicks from crossing that line, the line that everyone knows is there but so few venture beyond.

The problem is that every time you cross it, you have to step further beyond to get the same rush. And April had her limits. She wasn't into drugs, she did drink her share, she was okay with sex and sexuality, and she didn't really enjoy sex that much, at least from what she knows of it, but it was a useful tool, and it was a means to an end. She could really make people do things for her with the mere suggestion of physical gratification. It was somehow intoxicating.

She looked at her phone. 8:27 am. There was still time for her to get to school. Perhaps today, she will grace them with her presence.

She stopped filling her head with busy thoughts for a moment and flashed back to her mom's crying face, her split lip, and her bruised cheek. She shook her head to try to clear the memory.

...

There's Noah.

April waves. She's happier to see him than she expected she would be. Looking rumpled as usual, he's lumbering his way to school with his preppy shirt, his crazy hair with the cowlick in the back, and those timberland boots. Something about him makes her feel comfortable, and that's what she needs right now.

He puts his arm around her shoulders and pulls her in tightly.

"How have you been, babe?" he says casually.

"Good," April lied. "Really good."

Chapter 8
Things Are Good

James and Tori had gone on about five dates now, and James was allowing himself to feel something bordering on happiness. Probably not the joy that others feel, but for him, it was a start. Tonight, at Pizza Hut, he really let his guard down and let her in just a little.

I could get used to this, he thought.

But then he reminded himself of just who he is, how undeserving of this kind of satisfaction he is, and pulled himself back from his euphoria.

Though Tori, still laughing at his stories in all the right places, looking at him with a kind of admiration…maybe it could work.

James thought back to the night, now a month or more past. He walked into the liquor store with an excuse to buy some cigarettes and maybe a pack of gum. But really, he was interested in finding out just what her level of interest was. God knows she sent him all the right signals; this should be a lay-up for him.

He let her make the first move as she usually did. She asked him about the weather, of course, the hockey game, his work, whatever small talk that wouldn't stand out too much, not forcing her to take a risk. He let her go on for a while, then, out of the blue, he made his move.

"Hey, you wanna get coffee sometime?" he asked confidently and nonchalantly.

And that was it. Two days later, they're at that coffee shop on Second, the one that James kind of hated that was staffed by those two smug elitist women he thought might be sisters. They were always looking at him like his coffee money wasn't good enough for them.

Fuck them, he thought. Dunkin' Donuts coffee is better and a quarter the price. Cunts.

But today was different.

"You want to get a sandwich or something?"

He eyed the menu. $7.25 for an egg sandwich. How do they dare charge that?

Fast forward a month, and he's walking home from her place after the Pizza Hut date. James loved that pan pizza. And the salad bar with pepperoncini peppers. Those big red plastic cups that you could just keep sending back with the waitress for unlimited refills. The red and white checkered tablecloths. Pizza Hut was one of his favorite places to eat.

He's walking home and thinking about, of all things, his father.

James's father, an immigrant whose family escaped from behind the Iron Curtain. His dad was relatively young at the time but was shaped irrevocably by the stories his own father told: the knock on the door in the middle of the night, the secret police who would cart you off for no reason at all, the jackboots who would search your house, toss your belongings and take what they wanted. Everyone was helpless to stop them. No bystanders would dare say a word to them. Your neighbors would look the other way. Good friends and passing acquaintances would pretend they didn't know you. Tremendous injustice would be visited upon you, and you had no recourse whatsoever. You'd be forced to rot for a 'tenner' in inhumane conditions, cut off from any form of civilization in the labor camps.

That's why James's father always told him to keep a shotgun behind the door just in case he ever needed one. If more people in his country had armed themselves or were permitted to arm themselves, there would have been fewer of these late-night abductions.

...

James walked into his own front door. Glancing behind the

open door, he could see his own twelve-gauge pump-action double-barreled shotgun propped up against the wall. He hadn't touched it since he placed it there some nine years ago, but each time his gaze fell upon it, he would think of his father. That bastard.

James looked at the clock on his VCR. It was 9:45. Still too early to go to bed, but he kind of wanted to end the evening on a high note. He walked to the kitchen and poured himself the last glass from the Jameson bottle, the one he bought the last time he had a guest in his house.

"Guess I'll have to stop by the liquor store tomorrow," he said to no one. "I think Tori will be there when I get off work."

His mind drifted to Tori. Maybe it's time to invite her back here after a date and take things to the next level.

Just then, a cold sweat broke out on his forehead.

"I've got to scour this place for any evidence of anything."

A purse, a wallet, lipstick, a fake fingernail, bloodstains, rope, anything that would belie the careful image that James has been constructing for Tori.

He grabbed another contractor bag from the big yellow box in the basement. Starting at the ground floor, he began grabbing anything that was questionable and tossing it in the bag. There were a surprising number of incriminating items just lying around his house.

He made a note for himself for tomorrow to pick up one of those 2.5-gallon containers of all-purpose cleaner, Aisle 64 Bay E4, and scour this place from top to bottom, kind of like how those crime scene cleanup companies do it. He could do without the clean suit, though, if he needed one, there were plenty of options by the paint aisle.

After the cleanup, perhaps an update of the furniture and the television may be in order. The house really hasn't changed in the nine years since his mother went to that retirement community. And honestly, she probably hadn't changed things for at least fifteen years prior to that.

There was a sadness in the place that he had never really

noticed until he started looking at things through the eyes of a stranger. Well, not a stranger, but someone who had never been there before. And someone who would come there willingly and want to come back a second time.

There's so much to do, James thought.

He started dragging furniture to the door, down the porch steps, and out to the street. Going out the front door, he noticed a tear in the screen.

Chapter 9
With Great Responsibility Comes Great Power

Wednesday. 7 pm.

Richard should be at home right now, but he's not. He's sitting on a barstool at the corner of the bar.

It's not The Corkscrew; he won't be going back there for a while, if ever. Tonight, he's at Max's two blocks down and across the street.

Same drink, the same avoidance of the life that keeps hemming him in. Different dingy locations, different bartenders.

But now, he has to try harder at work, he thinks, stewing about his earlier talk with Albert.

Richard hates his job. He's not even sure of what he's supposed to be doing there, what value he is adding. Exactly how is he going to get better results when he struggles to understand the monthly reports? He thinks of that new guy, Joe. He seems to get it. Why do these things come so quickly to a jerk like that, and Richard has to expend so much more energy just to keep up? It's not fucking fair.

Could he talk with Joe? Maybe find out a missing piece to this puzzle? No, that would just open Richard up to further ridicule and make it clear that he didn't belong there. Belonging, this was a critical theme in Richard's life. Being part of an immigrant family, it was always important to belong. But what did that mean? Belong.

In the early years, it meant losing the accent, learning English, dressing the same as the others, wearing his hair the same, to kind of blend in with his classmates. Richard was never able to fully become accepted by his peers, either in school or in his life today. Sure, he met and married an American woman, had a house in the suburbs, went to the backyard cookouts, and drove a big, American car, but he was never comfortable with the small talk, the superficiality of suburban life. Richard always felt like something was not quite right like there was a hole in his being.

Now there was an imminent timeline, a ticking clock. He had six months to turn things around at work. On a shorter timescale, he needed to talk with his wife about the unresolved argument last night and, indeed, the new argument from tonight when he once again comes home drunk, smelling of alcohol and cigarettes, though he doesn't smoke. He still needs to do something about his right hand, which pains him every time he opens or closes his fist, which he has found himself frequently doing lately. He was not sure if it was a stress reaction or if the physical pain reminded him of the transcendent experience he had in that dirty bar bathroom last night.

Easier to just stay here and keep 'em coming.

He looked around the bar. Max's was more of a dive, a disreputable place that the college kids avoided. This absence of youth and enthusiasm left the place feeling a little more depressing, and its dated décor from the Eisenhower era certainly didn't help.

His eyes drifted to the crumpled-up bills in front of him on the bar. He had enough there for two more drinks, and he was going to make them last.

Hours later, Richard exited the bar in a fog, slightly stumbling up the three steps to the sidewalk level. The chilly autumn air was clearing his head a little.

He was furiously working up the rebuttal to last night's disagreement, telling her how things were going to change around the house, how he was not going to be taken for granted anymore, how he, the breadwinner, was going to call the shots and how the few dollars a week that she brought home from her hourly work at the local library was nice but was not life-changing and that she should know exactly who is in charge.

He would no longer tolerate her constantly reminding him of her need for intimacy and how she, continually telling him that he should touch her the way a husband touches his wife, was unwelcome advice. He would make it clear how he is comfortable with the way things are, and that's not going to change. Well, he's not exactly comfortable, but he's not in a position to blow up his life. He'll just soldier on, keep going through the motions, not letting the enormity of the mistakes he's made pile up around him until everything eventually just goes away.

He fumbled with his keys and the car door. Sliding behind the wheel of the LeSabre, he thought about taking a slow drive through the park, but no. He needs to get home, to face the music, as it were.

Driving as though on autopilot, he navigated the neighborhood streets and saw Bob and Mary's house.

Wonder how that therapy is going, guys? Have you resolved all of your animosity toward each other? No more fantasizing about a life without the other.

There was the stop sign again, the one at Maple and Pine, the decision that is really not a decision at all but an inevitable surrender to the left turn back to the life of quiet desperation.

The gentle rise of the driveway, the weed-choked gardens, the screen door. His "wife." The argument.

And here's Richard again, licking his wounds. Tonight's discussion with his wife went as badly as the one with Albert earlier today. What is it about his resolve? He was so confident of his position, so sure of himself coming into the conversation, and immediately his knees buckled, his spine collapsed, and he was mouthing the words that he would try to do better moving forward. Alone in the dark living room, with no blue light from the television, Richard took stock of his life.

How is it that there is not a single soul in the world that I can impose my will on? Why does no one recognize the power that resides within me? I come from a long line of proud men who stood tall. Of course, they spent years groveling under the iron thumb of communist oppression, but still, they were proud and tall. What would my father think of the man that I've become, this pathetic person sitting alone here in the dark?

How am I going to get my fire back? Where will I find the strength I've been missing for so fucking long? How am I going to learn to exercise my will on others? What is the solution to this dilemma that has been plaguing me?

Just then, he heard a crashing sound from his son's room. A light went on.

Chapter 10
A Life Forever Changed

Exhausted after a long night of work, James lay in bed, eyes wide open from the excitement, 2:45 am glowing on the clock on the nightstand.

James imagined Tori coming to his house, letting her guard down, becoming more comfortable, and letting him in. He was happy and, for once, in a good place.

Fatigue was creeping in, causing his defenses to slip. His mind began drifting to that dark place again. He thought back to the first time that it happened. It was late at night; he had been sleeping. He partially woke to the sound of his parents arguing but began drifting off again. He clumsily reached for a drink that he kept on his nightstand, the fog of sleep clouding his coordination. He knocked the glass to the floor, ice cubes and water splashing in all directions.

His father, lumbering up the stairs, muttering something unintelligible for the slurring. Jimmy was apologizing already before his father had fully ascended. There was something off with his manner, an aggressiveness he had not seen before.

Little Jimmy had already cleaned up all the ice cubes and was soaking up the spill with his bath towel when his father's silhouette darkened the doorway. Entering the room, his dad sat down on the bed, which was strange. In all of his eleven years, he could not remember his father entering his room, let alone sitting on the bed. His dad patted the covers, beckoning for him to have a seat. He felt his father's hand on the back of his neck, pulling him closer.

He was strong. Jimmy could not resist, and as much as he fought, he could not keep from losing his balance. Try as he might, he could not maintain any separation between his father and himself.

Hugging at first, more tightly than was comfortable, he then felt his father's hands invading his body. Confused, Jimmy closed his eyes tightly and allowed things to happen to him.

…

He had to stop thinking and get these images out of his head.

James sprung from the bed like a shot and found himself in the kitchen liquor cabinet without recalling how he got there. The bottle of whiskey had already found its way into his hand.

That was it, the point where his life had changed forever. His world came crashing down around him. Everything that he had relied on to this point was gone. His father, though never involved in his life, at least had never hurt him. That all changed. His mother, who had always been an advocate for him, left him totally exposed, in danger, and in harm's way.

Why didn't she do more to protect him?

She never intervened. She knew what was going on, night after night, and she did nothing.

I didn't deserve that, James thought. What did I know? I was just a kid!

Hiding under my covers, hoping he would just walk by. Maybe too drunk or tired to bother with me this night. It was always the same. The sweaty, smelly breath, the reek of cigarettes. The rough feel of his stubbly face over my smooth, eleven-year-old body.

"STOP IT!"

Gulping whiskey straight from the bottle, James thought about the subsequent years. Late middle school, where he had given up showering until his mother demanded he cleans himself up at least once a week. His greasy hair and skin, his face erupting in pimples, and his teeth that had not been brushed in days, were all defense mechanisms to protect him from those late-night intrusions. He was creating a protective shell of filth around him to keep his father's lecherous tendencies at bay. These habits had the undesirable side effect of ostracizing him from his peers, friends, and, of course, girls.

Small price to pay, Jimmy thought if it would make his father stop. But that bastard didn't stop. He would never stop.

Each day in school, he would avoid eye contact and slouch in the corner of the classroom, believing firmly that the whole school knew his horrible secret. He began to resent all these kids, with their effortless lives and their absence of abuse at home. He would listen to them lament about how strict their parents were and how stupid someone's dad was. Jimmy yearned for problems like these.

This was Jimmy's life for years. For him, the frustration, isolation, and desperation reached a boiling point in the tenth grade. The abuse at home, abuse from his cohorts at school, and the lack of support from any power structure within the school. Miss Jennings, the guidance counselor, spent more time flirting with the school's standout athletes than worrying about Jimmy's future. Reliving some bizarro world high school experiences that she never had. The cunt.

Something's got to change, thought Jimmy. How can he make this horror end?

Jimmy worked out the details in his head. He'd bring his dad's old revolver to school with all six chambers loaded and two boxes of ammunition; .357 is what it took. Jimmy had to look this up. Between what was in the gun and what was left in the two boxes, he'd have fifty rounds. He practiced loading and unloading the gun so he could do it quickly but hadn't actually fired the gun because the ammo is kind of expensive for a fifteen-year-old, and he couldn't have the gun smelling of gunpowder in his dad's desk drawer.

He'd go to his locker before lunch and retrieve the weapon, conceal it in the small of his back under his jacket until he reached the cafeteria. He'd burst through the doors and yell.

What is it that he would yell?

Something that would make them all understand. Make them see that he wasn't the freak that they all thought he was. He will need to work on the details of the final utterance.

Anyway, he'd yell what he figured to yell and then start shooting. Not sure who would get the first shot. Matt probably. That kid Matt. What a dick. Whatever he yelled had to be short and meaningful; screaming would start, and then gunfire, and everything would go haywire, so it had to be quick and direct, and straightforward. Nothing worse than one of the survivors misunderstanding what it was that you said, repeating it to the police incorrectly after you were gone, and everyone thinking you meant something other than what you actually meant.

For months, people would be asking themselves or others in the discussion, what do you think Jimmy meant by that? Why would he kill people over something so minor? Stuff like that. No, it had to be precise. Maybe he could write it down just to be sure that the message got out there so that after he used the last bullet on himself, the investigators could discover the message that he really wanted to convey.

Boothe had it right.

"Death to Tyrants!"

Or, more precisely, "Thus always to Tyrants!" the thus being Abraham Lincoln's shattered skull and a mixture of blood and cerebrospinal fluid leaking out all over the floor.

But then he had to go and say it in Latin. That must have been alienating for the Ford Theater audience. The point is no one would question John's intent. The message was short and sweet, uttered with a dramatic flourish.

Jimmy would have to work on that as well. The flourish.

So, empty the gun at everyone who scorned him, ridiculed him, or ignored him. Shake the spent cartridges loose, refill the chambers, and empty them again.

Wash, rinse, repeat.

Keep track of the bullets, save the last one for himself, and go out in dramatic fashion. Six times eight, that's forty-eight bullets, eight reloads; though his hands may be shaking, he might drop some on the floor, he'll probably have to keep moving to ensure that no brave hero types can intervene and save the day. Maybe keep one in his pocket just to be sure he isn't caught or captured.

The shooting will prompt an investigation, and maybe Mom will talk to the police and let them know what drove me to this. Jimmy's home life and environment will need to be inspected. People will demand answers.

Maybe I write about my father in the note with my dying declaration. My dad would get arrested and thrown in the slammer, where he can never do this again. I guess either way; I'll never suffer that indignity again.

The big day arrives, and Jimmy checks his backpack. Got the pistol, got two boxes of Remington High Terminal Performance .357 magnum rounds, 158-grain sp.

Not sure what the sp means, but I'm sure these will do the job. Wait, sp means soft-point. He remembered his dad telling him about that. Maybe he should have gotten the hp version.

Oh well, no matter.

Sitting in class was hell all morning, staring at the clock and waiting for the lunch bell. Getting his affairs in order. Mental affairs that is. He's just a teenager. No need for life insurance, a will, or any of those things.

"Is there an afterlife?" he asked himself. If so, I guess it's eternal damnation for me."

That's okay; he could live with it.

…

Gazing out the window on this spring morning, he sees new growth sprouting on the trees, flowers opening on the dogwood in front of Mr. Saylor's office, and birds frolicking about the bushes across the school's driveway.

"Jimmy?"

"Wha-what?" he stammers as the rest of the class laughs at him, caught daydreaming.

We'll see who is laughing later. Jimmy's inner monologue calmly reassures him.

"Do you know what Paul meant when he said, 'I do not belong here any- more; it is a foreign world.'?"

They were reading All Quiet on the Western Front this semester. Jimmy didn't really care to follow along with it. He hated reading, hated anything that required him to sit still and think.

"Honestly, Mrs. Romano, I don't fucking care," Jimmy said aloud, to the delight of his classmates.

There was an uproar throughout the room, and before he knew it, Jimmy was on his way to the principal. He would get a closer view of those dogwood blooms from across Mr. Saylor's desk.

This whole experience took the wind out of Jimmy's murder/ suicide plans, and thirty-five or so kids would live to see another day.

You're fucking welcome.

Jimmy's dad visited him later that night.

Chapter 11
To Feel Something, Anything

Another song is queued up on April's streaming service. This song is really old. It's a melancholy tune that touches her heart.

"Did you write the book of love? And do you have faith in God above…"

It's all about a plane crash that killed some famous musicians, along with a kind of oral history of music from the 70s. She intends to look into the other artists referenced in the song, but she keeps getting distracted.

The song takes her away to a simpler time, where there is good and bad, right and wrong. It's a relief from this world of gray she lives in now.

She thinks about the autobiographical tale of the singer, an innocent child delivering newspapers and feeling a sense of loss for people he has never met and does not know. April finds that she is crying, and she's not sure exactly why.

Untimely death has been somewhat of a fascination for April. She thinks about the "27 Club", a group of creatives, artists, musicians, and other famous people who checked out in their 27th year. What a luxury for these people to die while on the way up… young, beautiful, and leading a life full of possibilities. She thinks of some of the rock personalities of today that may have benefited from joining this club. Looking at Steven Tyler on the panel of judges for *American Idol* or seeing pictures or YouTube videos of "Fat Elvis,"…she thinks that's another one that could have benefited from an early exit. How embarrassed would their young selves be by what they became?

Ted Nugent, at twenty-seven, had released his first solo

album.

This record gave the world *Stranglehold, Motor City Madhouse, Stormtroopin,* and more. If he punched his ticket somewhere after that release, he would be lionized today. Sure, we would never have known *Cat Scratch Fever or Free-for-All,* but that's a fair trade for the embarrassing joke that "The Nuge" became. Being all right-wing and firing automatic weapons on stage, shooting bow and arrows into the crowd, living off of fifty-year-old songs.

Human beings are intended to have a limited run on this earth. It is said the light that burns twice as bright burns half as long. Perhaps the spotlight, throngs of adoring fans, and being surrounded by people serving at your pleasure causes one to lose their grounding.

Michael Jackson, another perfect example, "The King of Pop," turned twenty-seven in 1985, three years after releasing *"Thriller,"* his crowning achievement. Had he OD'd on Propofol in 1985, sure, we would never have heard *"Bad," "The Way You Make Me Feel,"* or *"Smooth Criminal,"* but we also wouldn't have heard about sleepovers with young boys at the Neverland Ranch. Again, the celestial scales are balanced.

Who would doubt that forty-year-old Jim Morrison would have become an unbearable asshole, sullying his reputation and diminishing his contribution to rock history?

Would anyone want to see a fat, balding Kurt Cobain, once the iconoclastic rebel, becoming the very establishment that he railed against?

Courtney Love is another excellent candidate for the club. She hit twenty-seven on July 9th, 1991, after Hole had already released *Celebrity Skin, Live Through This,* and certainly after the studio work was done for *Pretty on the Inside.* She hasn't provided the world with anything of value since then. Her premature death would have most likely kept Cobain from joining the club since I'm 99% sure she murdered him, and it would spare me the commercials hearing her push auto-immune CBD oil medications after surviving a near-death experience with anemia.

Would Amy Winehouse be as loved today if she wandered around in an Ozzy-like stupor? Mumbling incoherently due to the brain damage that years of drug and alcohol abuse would undoubtedly have inflicted on her. Of course, the answer is "no," or should I say, "No, no, no…?"

It's important to know when to get out. Always leave them wanting more. These are words to live by.

April thinks about this as she slides a razor blade along the inside of her thigh, making tiny incisions in her skin, just deep enough to draw blood but not enough to cause any major injury. She feels an instant rush from the pain, a sense of control over something in her life.

She thinks of Noah, his kind face, his preppy style, his all-around niceness. He would hate that she is doing this. She used to cut on her wrists until her mom noticed the marks and, as a result, sent her to a therapist for a while. The therapy didn't help, but it made April start cutting in more discreet areas.

Noah had dramatically improved April's life in meaningful ways. They came together in a turbulent time for her; she had just been recovering emotionally from a traumatic experience. Having been raped by one of her mom's latest boyfriend/handymen, who thankfully and, surprisingly, her mom threw out, April had a hard time staying focused. She would begin crying hysterically, suddenly, and frequently. Sharing an almost identical class schedule with April, though really nothing else, Noah was witness to many of these breakdowns.

He was a gentle, soft shoulder for her to lean on, a shoulder with no agenda or designs. He was a kind and thoughtful soul who made her feel safe, made her feel like she was worth something.

Not like that asshole her mom inflicted on her. That old, dirty, smelly jerk whose hands were all over her neck, her face, in her mouth. The disgusting salty flavor of his thumb on her tongue. The choking sensation she felt when he wrapped his rough, cracked palms around her throat or put his hand over her mouth to silence her as he climbed on top of her. Noah would never do that. He is good to her. His soft hands provided a sense of warmth to her, not cold and prickly assaults on her body.

That is why she sometimes feels bad when she pushes him past his limits, like when she introduced him to blood play. He was so disgusted he wouldn't even look at her for several days. She began to feel so alone and isolated that she begged his forgiveness and said she'd never do that again. Things gradually got back to normal, only for her to push him into that restroom stall at the diner late one night, and he got mad at her all over again.

April didn't know why she did these things. Maybe deep down, she did not feel deserving of a love as pure as the love that Noah showed her and therefore was continually trying to push him away. Maybe she found him kind of stiff and boring in his niceness and was trying to draw something more out of him. Whatever the reason, this constant push/pull of tension allowed the otherwise casual relationship to fit more comfortably in April's life of tumult.

She knew the relationship would not last, but in her experience, nothing does, so why not soak in every comforting detail of it while it's still here? She could hear her mom's words echoing in her head.

She would get from it what she could until she didn't need him anymore.

Chapter 12
This Can't Go On

Things are deteriorating, thought James.

It's been several months since Tori moved in.

It was nice at first, but now he does not feel the electricity in her touch when she sits beside him on the couch or as they lay in bed. He feels she has invaded his space and he yearns for privacy. She never moved into the room without the door; she bypassed that together and joined him in his mom and dad's room. He was so excited at the time. His plans were coming together; someone saw what he could not see in himself.

The sex was adequate.

Of course, James was guarded. How could he not be after what was done to him as a child? Tori knew none of this.

How could she? He'd never reveal such an embarrassing secret. No, he'll take that to the grave. She was pretty timid about intimacy, the two of them discovering each other slowly, carefully. It was nice.

But that was months ago. Now Tori is focused elsewhere. Ever since it happened, she no longer stays up late and drinks with him. She pressures him to get a better job. She starts to nag him about the food that they eat. It's like his wishes don't exist in her mind, not how they used to.

Sure, he gets pissed. Who wouldn't? Occasionally, he feels terrible for his loss of temper. Like that time, she cracked her tooth. As usual, she started in on him again about this or that, and he hit her so hard that she fell face-first against the kitchen counter. That was bad. He'd hit her a few other times as well. It's just that she's so fucking selfish. She had to go and fuck everything up, and now

James was not sure what he should do. Granted, she's not down there screaming like the others, and really, he could just send her on her way; he didn't do anything illegal in this case. A little battery, but that would be he said/she said scenario, and he didn't leave too many marks. But she has a part of him now. What does that mean for the future?

Plus, she has changed. Where she used to be tiny, playful, and free-spirited…now she's getting rounder, and her feet are getting puffy. He doesn't like it. Rubbing her stomach all the time. Fucking bitch had to get pregnant.

It's all "we" and "when the baby comes…".

What about my needs, James thinks.

She doesn't care. It's all about this parasite growing inside her. Sapping her of the light that was in her eyes. Taking the joy out of everything.

He can see it. The way she looks at him now. Not like before. Not like when he would go into the liquor store and she would purposely touch his hand. She would hang on to his words and stare into his eyes. That has all changed now. As if the guy he was is no longer adequate for the changing landscape. Well, fuck her. What did she bring to this situation? He gave her a place to stay, a… well, lots of other stuff. And what does she do for me besides nag about the kitchen or the yard?

"A whole lot of nothing," he muses.

James downs more of his whiskey. The bottle is getting low. She's still at work. He should call and ask her to bring home another one.

No answer.

He'll just leave a message.

Almost out of Jameson, bring another bottle home with you. "Bitch."

…

"A girl," James mutters to himself. "What the fuck am I

supposed to do with a baby girl? A fucking girl."

He turned on the TV and flipped the channels for a while. There was nothing good on, nothing he wanted to see…the melodramatic news anchors going on about another fucking missing girl, Judge Judy calling someone a moron, a rerun of *The Joker's Wild* with Jack Berry…so he stopped at an old movie where Burt Reynolds was a cop somewhere down south. He'd seen this one before. I think Burt gets his fingers chopped off or broken or something. Not broken in that "Blade Runner" way, where the robot dude just grabs them and bends 'em the wrong way. Actually, it was kind of like that.

No, they get chopped completely off. Yow! that must hurt like a mother. In the end, Burt loses two fingers but gets the girl.

I'd keep my fingers and ditch the girl, thought James.

11 pm. She should be here by now.

"Where the fuck…"

Just then, he heard the sound of her car pulling into the driveway.

"About fucking time."

She came through the front door, kind of frazzled, like usual. She had a ritual every time she came home. Purse on the hook, keys in the basket, earrings and rings in the dish, and shoes on the little rack she got from Home Goods. That stupid rack. The shelf is eight inches wide. For shoes. How the hell are his size eleven shoes going to balance on that piece of the shit little rack? Then the pants come off, then the bra from under the shirt where her tits just fall down like they're tired of her, too.

"How was your day?" she asks.

"You get my bottle?"

"What bottle?" Tori asks him innocently.

"Fucking figures." James retorts. "I left you a message, and you couldn't do this one thing for me?"

"Sorry, I didn't notice. By the way, Susan and Russ want us to come over on Saturday. Are we doing anything?"

"Sure, you won't show up at Susan and Russ' empty-handed," James responded pettily.

"Babe, I'm sorry I didn't get you more whiskey. I didn't notice that you called, okay? I'm working the early shift tomorrow. I'll make sure to bring a bottle home then. I'll probably even beat you home from work tomorrow."

"That's not the point!" James replies indignantly.

"What is the point then if it's not the whiskey?" "It's how you focus all your attention on that stupid baby. How everything has changed, how no one cares about my needs anymore."

"Do you honestly think I wanted to get pregnant? This is the last thing that I want. I'm already dealing with one baby in this relationship…"

…

James flew across the room and slapped her before she could even finish the sentence. She staggered back, but he grabbed her shoulders and pulled her toward him. Simultaneously, he stuck his leg, judo-style, between them and threw her to the ground, just inches away from the front door. He climbed on top of her, feeling her swollen belly below him as he straddled her, exerting complete control.

He put one hand on her forehead and the other under her chin, orienting her face so she was staring directly into his eyes which were inches from hers, as he loomed over her prostrate form.

"WHO IS THE BABY?!" he screamed directly into her face, spit flying from his mouth as his eyes flared in a manner indicating that James had taken leave of his senses.

"WHO IS THE FUCKING BABY?!" he repeated, firmly slamming the back of her head into the floor.

"Stop it; you're hurting me!" Tori pleaded.

One more slam against the floor, and then James moved his hand from her forehead to her neck.

We're back here again, James thought.

It's already gone too far; she could call the cops, and I'd do time for abuse. There would be an investigation; unwanted evidence could be discovered, and this could all come crashing down. I'm so stupid. How did I let this into my life? I did this to myself; it's the only way.

James placed both hands around her neck and started to lean in with the entirety of his body weight. Tori scraped and clawed at his arms and face, sputtering and spitting just like he remembered that other girl doing before he incorporated the drugs into his routine. Her body thrashed below him, unable to dislodge him from his control position.

Tori's hands fell to her side, still scrambling around, her consciousness fading. Her right hand brushed up against something hard. She looked to her right and saw that stupid cast iron doorstop from the thirties. James' mom liked that thing, so he would never throw it away despite Tori's requests. A creepy-looking rabbit with ridiculous floppy ears.

She grabbed it in her fist and swung at his head with all her might.

James was thinking about how sad he was going to be after disposing of Tori's body, looking into the eyes that were rolling back in her head, remembering the first few dates, how he was walking on air on his way home. Listening to her gurgle and choke for breath instead of the sound of her laughter and calling out his name.

He closed his eyes, not wanting to remember her this way, when he saw a flash of light through his closed eyes and felt something like a hammer colliding with his temple.

Both his arms went limp, and he fell face first, his head bouncing off the floor.

With his weight shifting forward, Tori was able to squeeze out from under him and back her way to the door, pulling her knees to her chest for protection.

James, already quite drunk and doubly impaired by the shot to the side of the head, began to vomit on the linoleum floor of the foyer. The orangish-red mixture of the whiskey and the chicken parm he had earlier clashed with the bluish-green flower pattern of the floor.

Tori had only seconds to compose herself. She knew he'd recover and redouble his efforts to kill her. Glancing around, she saw James' dad's shotgun just inches to her right. Reaching out confidently, she grabbed the weapon and placed its stock against her shoulder. Racking the action, she heard a shell enter the chamber. James heard it, too, and whirled around quickly to look at her. He found Tori pointing a gun directly at him, only six feet away.

"Oooh...look at the little girl with the big gun," he said derisively. "What are you going to do? Shoot me?"

"I don't want to shoot you, but you just tried to kill me," Tori said, her voice cracking. Let me...let me just...grab a few things... and...I will get out of here, and...you...you won't ever hear from me again."

Tori's voice was shaking as much as her hands were, struggling to grip the gun.

"You don't even hold that thing properly," James taunted, his eyes practically glowing red.

"Look, I...I...I don't know what set you off tonight, and frankly, I don't care. But... I am not going to die here tonight. I'm not. I'd prefer it if you didn't die either, but that...that decision is totally up to you. Now...let... let me get some clothes and things and let me go, or so help me God, I will fucking gun you down right here on the spot."

James thought about it for a moment.

No chance she doesn't go to the cops if I let her out of here.

I don't think she's ever fired a gun in her life.

"Okay," he told her, smiling. "Get what you need and get the fuck out."

...

Tori lowered the gun.

James lunged toward her.

Instinctively, she raised the shotgun and pulled both triggers. A deafening blast rang out.

...

Tori slumped to the floor once again and pulled her knees back to her chest. James' labored breathing was slowing. Tears streamed down her cheeks as she wailed into her legs. She looked at her watch. 11:25 pm, April 14th.

Sic semper tyrannis...

Chapter 13
The Send-Off

April's head was spinning. She looked at the clock on the wall. She had been in the same seat more or less since 9 am if you don't count the five-minute break at 10 am and then the more luxurious ten-minute break just an hour later. Roughly an hour to go, and she wasn't sure she had gotten a single question correct yet. She was seriously regretting her decision to take the SATs.

Noah was taking the test as well. He was just two rows ahead and three seats to the right. Didn't appear to be breaking a sweat. But why should he? He was already as good as accepted to Princeton as a legacy, his father having been a standout student in some sort of engineering there. He scored 1480 the last time he took the test; he's just trying to boost his score a bit to make the application look better.

Me, on the other hand, I'll be lucky to score a 400. Wonder what the minimum SAT score the local community college will allow?

She looked back at the test, trying to focus on the words:

Aaron is staying at a hotel that charges $99.95 per night plus tax for a room. A tax of 8% is applied to the room rate, and an additional one-time untaxed fee of $5.00 is charged by the hotel. Which of the following represents Aaron's total charge, in dollars, for staying x nights?

Who the fuck is Aaron, and what is he doing at this hotel? I don't think I've ever stayed a single night in a hotel in my life. And, if I did, would I be standing at the front desk checking the numbers in my head? Like, is this how hotels make extra money or something by trying to rip off people who aren't good at math? What do I need to know this shit for?

"Fuck this. I'm out."

She slammed the test booklet closed, hastily grabbed her stuff, walked to the front of the room, and threw the test at the proctor while hustling out the door. She crumpled to a bench in the lobby and began to cry as she waited for Noah to exit the test when he was actually finished with it, as the responsible students do.

April is to Noah as…blank is to blank, April thought. Let's see…as a tick is to its host? That is a strong contender. Chicken fingers is to Filet Mignon? Another good one. How about a tricycle is to a Ferrari? I'm going to go with "D," all of the above.

…

Forty-five minutes later, Noah strolled confidently out of the testing room with a concerned look on his face. He gave April a hug, and despite his concerned expression, he couldn't help but flash her a warm and comforting smile.

"It's going to be okay," he said.

She didn't respond.

"Plus, it's just about noon on a Saturday," Noah continued, hopeful that he was striking a good chord. "We have the whole weekend ahead of us."

He was right, of course. No reason to get too upset about the SATs. Even if she aced it, it was a long shot for her to get accepted into a college and then actually be able to attend. Her mom had not saved any money for her education. She could take loans, but would she ever be able to pay them back? Hell, she had to borrow fifty bucks from Noah just to register for this test today…the one she bombed so spectacularly.

"I'll get you your fifty dollars back," she said. "Don't worry."

"Oh, don't worry about it," he replied.

April got into his car, the disaster of the SATs already fading from her thoughts. Her mind had shifted focus to this evening's plans. She and Noah were driving up the New Jersey Turnpike to the First National Bank Center to see a Post Malone show. She had been waiting months for this day to arrive.

April arrived home to an empty house. Noah couldn't stay; he said he had things to do, so she began to make preparations for the evening. Pick out her clothes, pack some supplies, take a quick power nap, shower, and get ready for the show of a lifetime.

She raided the kitchen cabinets for any portable foodstuffs she could find. Then over to the liquor cabinet.

"What won't Mom miss?"

She found an old dusty bottle of Jameson in the back corner. She threw that in her backpack, wondering if it was still drinkable. It was that old. She never remembered her mother drinking Jameson…

Then to her closet for an outfit. Dresses, jeans and, a shirt, leggings. She ended up with a loose and flowy summer dress, even though it was a little early for the season.

Wonder if it will be too cold?

She threw in a cardigan and some knee-high boots, just in case. The First National Bank Center was one of those indoor/ outdoor venues. Had a stage at the bottom of a gentle hill with a half-moon of about 7,000 seats in front of the stage. Then on the grassy hill behind the seats, there is room for another twelve or so thousand concertgoers with general admission seating on the ground, on blankets, on those stupid fold-up camp chairs, or on the more stupid mini beach chairs. April and Noah sprang for reserved seating for this show. You never know what to expect from general admission. They got good seats, too, in Section A.

April tried to tamp down her excitement, but it was hard.

2:00…she had time to nap for an hour, so she set the alarm on her phone, set a second alarm for five minutes later, and, just to be safe, texted her friend, Ruth, and asked her to call at 3:15 to be triply sure.

She lounged on the couch, put some background noise on the TV, and tried to quiet her mind. Putting the thoughts and uncertainties of the day behind her.

If Noah goes to an Ivy League school an hour and a half away, how many minutes will it take him to forget about April and find a new, rich, more suitable girlfriend?

Burying her face in the pillow, she tried to shut out these thoughts. Failing at that task, she walked to the bathroom and reached in her makeup case for the razor blade that she had hidden in there.

…

She stirred to the annoying but lyrical chimes of her "waves" ringtone and groggily reached for her phone. Knocking it to the floor, she struggled to turn off the sound that was mocking her so cheerfully.

She sat up and noticed a little dried blood on the couch. Grabbing a rag, a dab of soap, and some cold water, she hurriedly cleaned up the cushion.

She texted Noah:

"Can't wait to see you tonight. I have booze! :)"

…and jumped into the shower. Shaving her legs even a little higher, she wanted to make sure that everything was going to be perfect tonight. Summer was coming, and she wanted to make the most of the last few months that she had with Noah before he left for school. April was determined to give him a send-off to college that he would never forget. Plus, she'd be doing things that those snotty Ivy League girls just wouldn't do.

On to getting dressed, styling her hair, and applying makeup. April tried to accentuate the best of her features.

Looking in the full-length mirror in her mom's room, she took in her appearance.

"Noah's a lucky man," she lied to herself.

Looking down at her phone, she texted:

"Ready whenever you are! "

She wasn't sure why she used the bomb emoji. In hindsight, it was a little dark. Maybe something about the fuse related to a countdown?

…

In Noah's car, approaching the Ben Franklin bridge, April could see dark clouds looming over the city. She felt an uneasy sense of foreboding. It had been raining on and off all day though tonight was more on than off. So glad they got the seats under the roof. Listening to "Beerbongs & Bentleys" on the CD player in Noah's car. His Toyota was just old enough to still have one of those but not new enough for Bluetooth.

April listened to the lyrics of the next song with a heavy heart.

"You prolly think that you're better now, better now. You only say that 'cause I'm not around, not around. You know I never meant to let you down, let you down. Woulda given you anything."

Gazing over the Delaware River, she asked, "What's going to happen to us when you go off to school?" and braced for the response.

"We'll have to see, babe…I don't know what to expect," Noah answered transparently.

…

"That's what I was afraid of."

They drove in silence for ten minutes, but it seemed more like an hour. Only the sound of the windshield wipers beating the streaming rain from the windshield, each swipe a thump like a beating heart.

Staring out the window, April watched the mile markers zip past as if they were ticking off the minutes that she had left with Noah.

Suddenly, April was overcome with the urge to make some kind of dramatic gesture, to indelibly write her image into Noah's brain for eternity.

She took a deep breath, unbuckled her seat belt, leaned over, and began undoing Noah's pants. He nervously asked what she thought she was doing and playfully fought her off. When his genitals were fully exposed, she threw her right leg over his lap, nearly missing the steering wheel. She pulled her panties to the side and lowered herself onto him.

Panicking, Noah responded excitedly, "April! What are you doing? I can't see!"

He pushed her by the shoulder, trying to force her back to her seat. April's backside hit the bottom of the steering wheel and jerked it sharply to the left. The car lurched 85 miles per hour, the wet road surface causing the Toyota to lift off the road and roll eastbound down two lanes of I-95.

Noah's sense of up and down was suddenly scrambled. He felt himself being tossed about to the limits of his seatbelt and shoulder strap. The shuddering sound of crunching metal and breaking glass claimed the aural space previously occupied by Post Malone.

After what seemed like an eternity, what was left of the car rolled slowly to a stop.

. . .

Opening his eyes and desperately trying to focus his view on the interior of the now smoke-filled vehicle, Noah could feel a wet and sticky substance covering his body. It was thick like syrup.

Epilogue

Noah was released from the hospital after twenty-four hours of observation. The combination of his seatbelt and the airbags protected him well. A few stitches from the broken glass and a cervical collar for safety were the sum total of the damage he suffered.

April was not so lucky. Her memorial would occur two days from now.

How could he go to the service? How can he face her mother and their friends from school?

He couldn't.

As the sole survivor of that fatal crash, the guilt and remorse overwhelmed him as he carefully relayed most of the details to his family. Noah's father stayed with him almost all of the twenty-four hours at the hospital. He informed Noah that the car, of course, was totaled. The police investigation found a bottle of liquor in the car, though Noah's blood tests at the hospital proved that he was sober at the time of the accident. He told police that a deer had run onto the highway, and he swerved to miss it. The actual story was too much for him to tell.

In the police report, the EMTs relayed the scene as they discovered it. Initially, they thought there was one occupant of the vehicle and desperately searched his body for the source of all the blood that had covered him. It was dark, still raining, and hard to piece together the events. Only later did they find April or parts of April. The service would have to be a closed casket.

Noah informed his father that he would like to go home, and upon arriving home, he went straight to his room and crawled into bed. The room lights were off, and the shades were down. Although not seriously injured, Noah's body hurt just about everywhere. He lay in bed for twelve hours or more. Often, his mom or dad would hover by the door.

"Noah, can we get you anything?"

"Do you want to talk"

"Are you ok?"

…

But this time, there was something different, more urgent about the gentle knock than usual. Noah's father cracked the door and stuck his head in.

"Noah…April's mother is here. She wants to talk to you."

…

"No, Dad. I can't see her right now. I don't want to talk to anyone. Please don't make me."

"Son," he said in his most paternal voice.

"She doesn't blame you. She just wants to talk. She needs to understand how her daughter was feeling in her last few moments."

…

"Take about ten minutes to collect yourself, and then come on down. We will be there to support you."

…

About fifteen minutes later, Noah emerged from his room and walked downstairs to find his mother and father talking with April's mom in the living room. There was a tray of snacks on the coffee table. And the mood seemed strangely light given the circumstances.

"Hi, Noah," April's mom said warmly. "I'm so sorry this happened to you."

"Sit down. Are you hungry?" Noah's mother asked. "Do you want something to drink?"

"No, I'm good," Noah said, his voice cracking from the

emotion. "Don't blame yourself for this," Tori said to Noah. "I always sort of suspected that April's life would end suddenly… tragically…like this."

Everyone in the room stared at her, surprised at how matter-of-factly she said this.

"Let me tell you about our lives," Tori began hesitantly.

She went on to explain how she believed that April's father, Tori's boyfriend, had suffered prolonged and traumatic abuse as a child, how this trauma shaped his reactions to everything, and how his brain was wired differently as a result of what she believed was repeated molestation. It caused him to overreact strongly to situations, a kind of fight-or-flight instinct that he constantly struggled with.

She then explained their tumultuous relationship that culminated with the physical altercation that led to Tori killing him in self-defense, how the police investigated the incident, and how she got probation based on the evidence in the apartment combined with the ligature marks on her neck and other bruises and defensive wounds.

Tori then went on to describe the first couple of years of April's life, how there were a series of men involved in their lives, some good, some bad, ultimately leading to April being brutally raped at a young age. This further trauma, on top of already questionable genetics, exacerbated a profound case of clinical depression.

April had been in therapy for years and had participated in self-harm behaviors as well as risk-taking and acting out. Tori tried to be there for her, but when April started dating Noah, Tori explained she was so happy that April found a good person. Someone who would be nice to her, with no strings attached. She saw a change in April. She was more optimistic, less sullen, thinking about the future.

Unfortunately, it was probably the future without Noah that led her to the behaviors that ultimately cost her her life. The cops on the scene were caring enough to clean up the report, heck many of them probably had daughters, but Tori knew some guys on the job and got the unofficial details from the accident.

The driver, a young man in his late teens, had the seat belt buckled, belt, and pants not. Young girl, late teens, unbuckled, unrestrained. Alcohol on the scene, in the girl, roads wet, high rate of speed…it didn't take an advanced degree to figure out why this one ended the way it did.

Tori made sure to again let Noah know that she did not blame him for what happened. Thanked him for making her daughter's final months more pleasant than her prior years had been.

It was a lot for Noah to take in. As Tori was leaving, Noah finally spoke.

"It's hard to believe that one man's selfish actions nearly fifty years ago could have such negative consequences to so many people even to this day."

"Yes, it is" Tori replied.

…

"I guess the cycle has ended," Noah said hopefully.

THE END

Whether it's your friends, family, or community, everyone needs someone to lean on.

If you don't know where to turn, you can text **HOME** to **741741**.

A volunteer Crisis Counselor with Crisis Text Line will be there for you. It's free and 24/7.

This story was not written from personal experiences, but I recognize that people may be struggling with similar situations to those of the characters in this story. If you or anyone you know is dealing with depression, or anxiety, causing self-harm, has been molested or is molesting, is in an abusive relationship or is an abuser, is considering suicide, or thinking of taking someone's life. Please, please, please find the help you need or help the person in need by contacting a crisis counselor.